MY 1ST GRAPHIC NOVEL

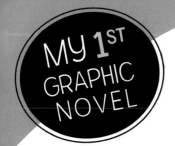

BELLA'S BOAT SURPRISE

My First Graphic Novels are published by Stone Arch Books
A Capstone Imprint
1710 Roe Crest Drive
North Mankato, Minnesota 56003
www.capstonepub.com

Library of Congress Cataloging-in-Publication Data
Jones, Christianne C.
    Bella's boat surprise / by Christianne C. Jones ; illustrated by Mary Sullivan.
    p. cm. — (My first graphic novel)
    ISBN 978-1-4342-1617-5 (library binding)
    ISBN 978-1-4342-2287-9 (softcover)
    1. Graphic novels. [1. Graphic novels. 2. Boats and boating—Fiction.]
I. Sullivan, Mary, 1958- ill. II. Title.
PZ7.7.J66Be 2010
[E]—dc22

                        2008053378

Summary: Bella is ready for her big boating adventure. She has everything she
needs. But will she be disappointed when she sees the boat her family picked?

Creative Director: Heather Kindseth
Graphic Designer: Hilary Wacholz

Printed in the United States of America in Stevens Point, Wisconsin.
010555R

MY 1ST GRAPHIC NOVEL

BELLA'S BOAT SURPRISE

by Christianne C. Jones
illustrated by Mary Sullivan

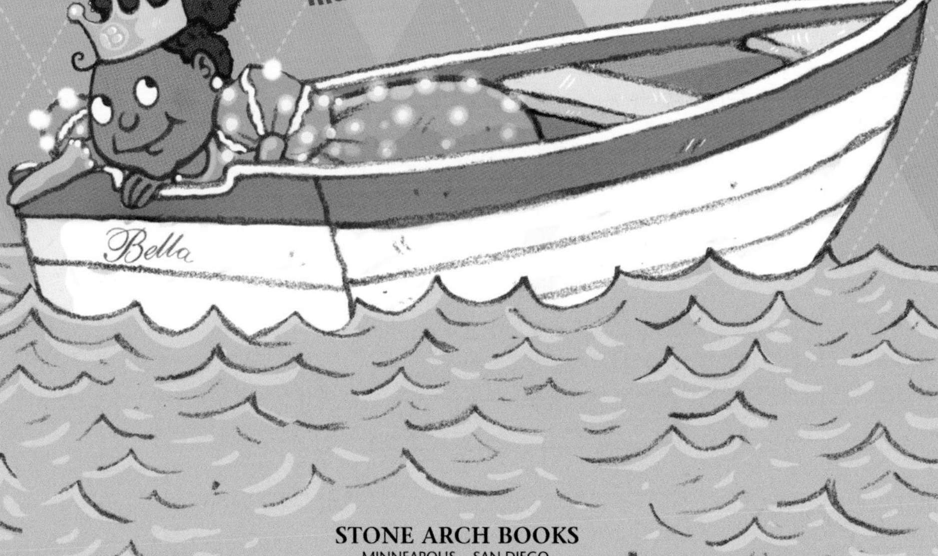
Bella

STONE ARCH BOOKS
MINNEAPOLIS SAN DIEGO

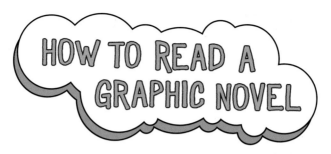

HOW TO READ A GRAPHIC NOVEL

Graphic novels are easy to read. Boxes called panels show you how to follow the story. Look at the panels from left to right and top to bottom.

Read the word boxes and word balloons from left to right as well. Don't forget the sound and action words in the pictures.

The pictures and the words work together to tell the whole story.

Bella had her new swimsuit on under her dress.

Oh, pretty.

Her hair looked perfect with her fancy sun hat.

Big sunglasses were the final touch.

Now I'm ready.

She grabbed her beach bag and ran out the door.

Bella was going on a boat, but that's all she knew.

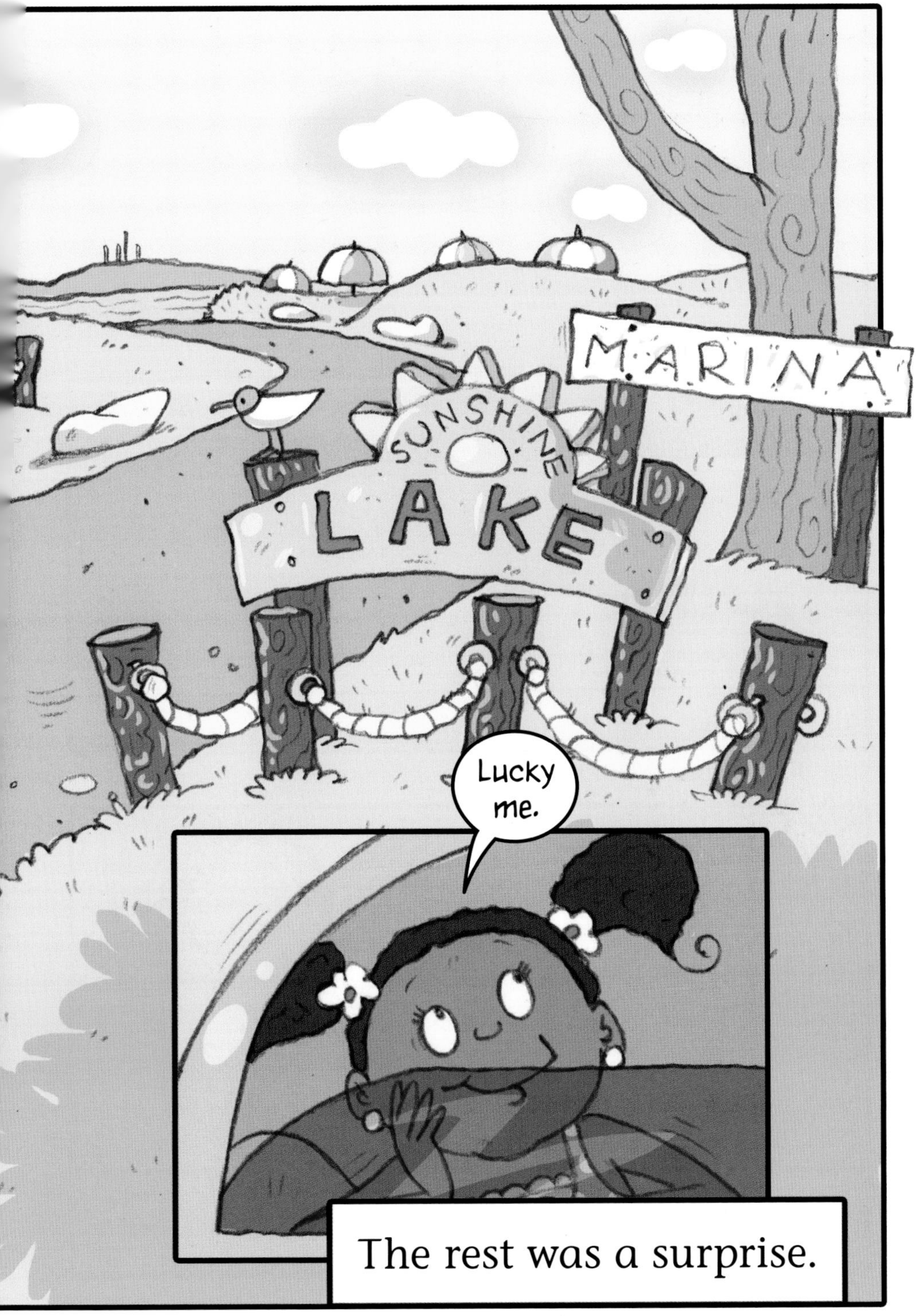
MARINA
SUNSHINE
LAKE
Lucky me.
The rest was a surprise.

Maybe it would be a cruise ship.

Bella would wear her best party dress.

She would eat lots of fancy foods.

Why, thank you!

She would dance to the big band.

Maybe it would be a rowboat.

Let me help you, miss.

Bella would wear her princess dress.

She would hold a fancy umbrella.

She would read her favorite book and watch the birds.

Maybe it would be a sailboat.

Bella would wear her sailor outfit.

She would help raise the sails.

Then she would relax under the sun.

When her family got to the dock, Bella didn't see any of her dream boats.

Instead, she saw a motorboat.

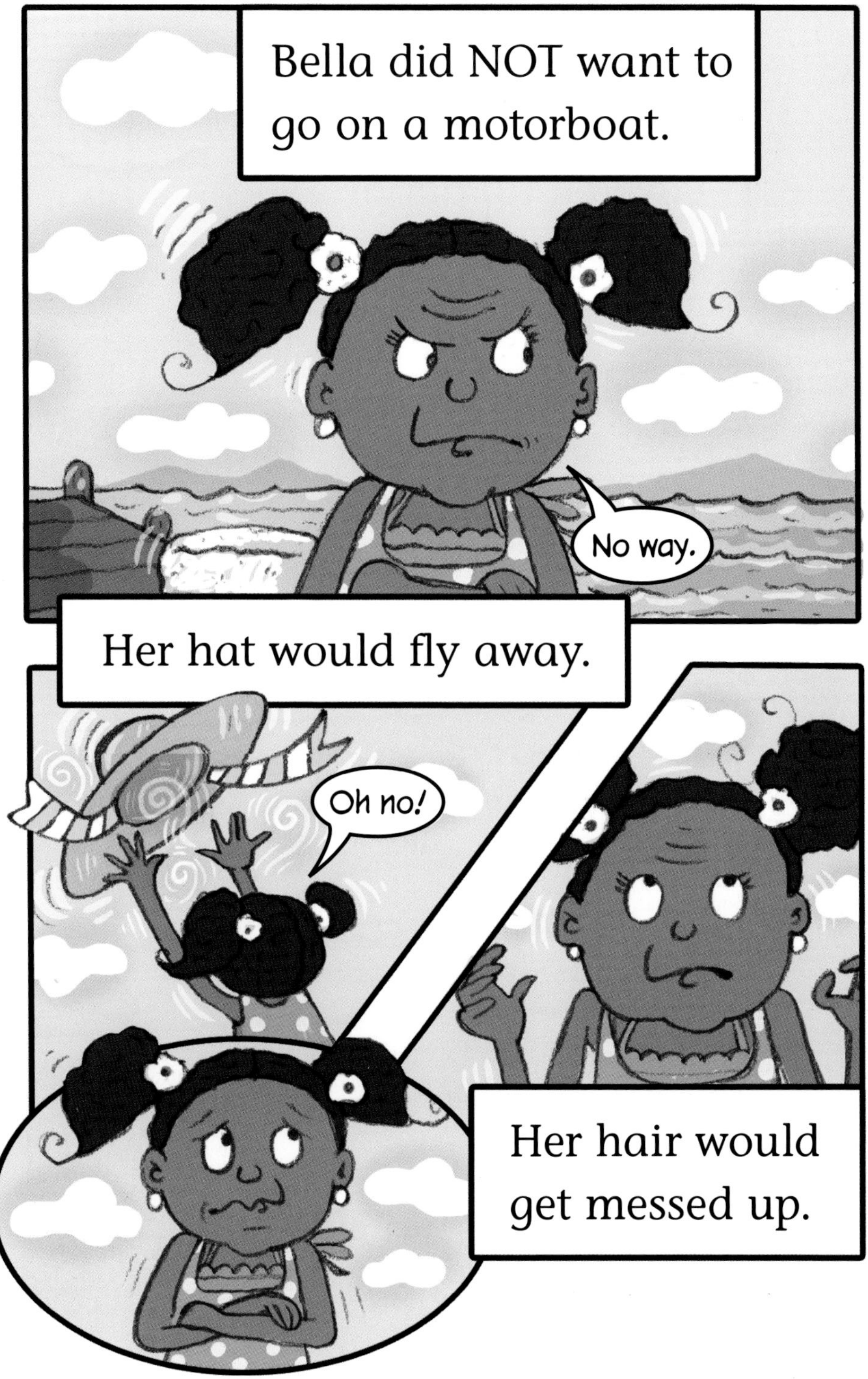
Bella did NOT want to go on a motorboat.
No way.
Her hat would fly away.
Oh no!
Her hair would get messed up.

Bella's parents made her put on a life jacket, which covered up her dress.

They sped out to the middle of the lake.

ZOOM

Hmph!

This was not going to be fun.

Bella's parents tied a tube to a rope.

Her brother jumped in and held the tube.

The tube hit wave after wave.

Her brother was yelling and smiling.

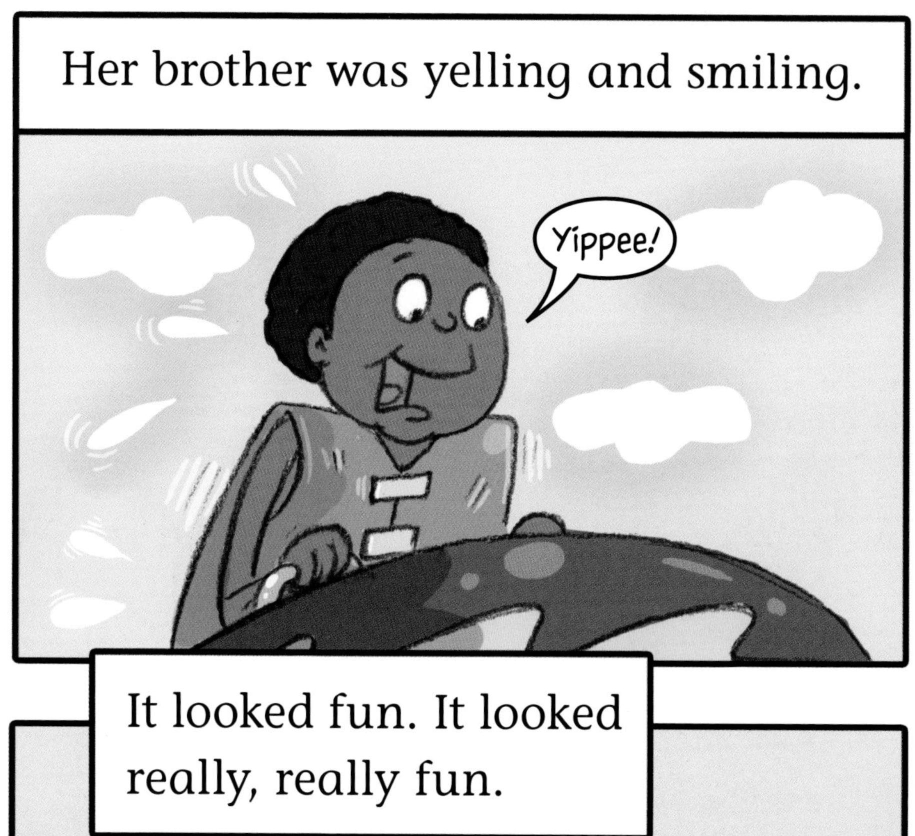
Yippee!

It looked fun. It looked really, really fun.

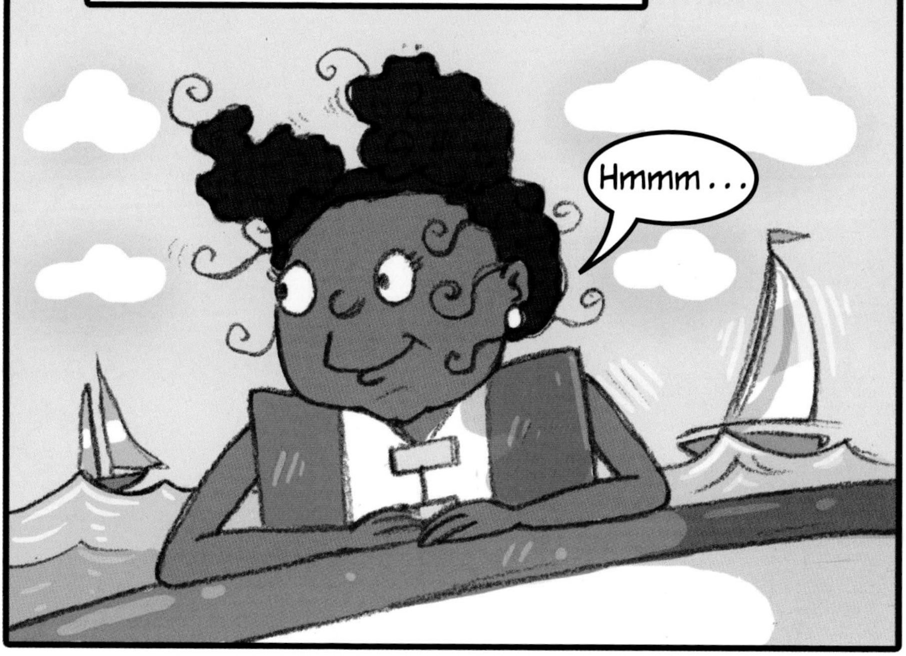
Hmmm . . .

Bella had to try it.

Maybe just once.

I'm already wet, and my hair is a mess!

22

Bella jumped in.

SPLASH!

Here I go!

She held the tube.

Wow!

She hit wave after wave.
She loved it!

At the end of the day, Bella was wet and tired.

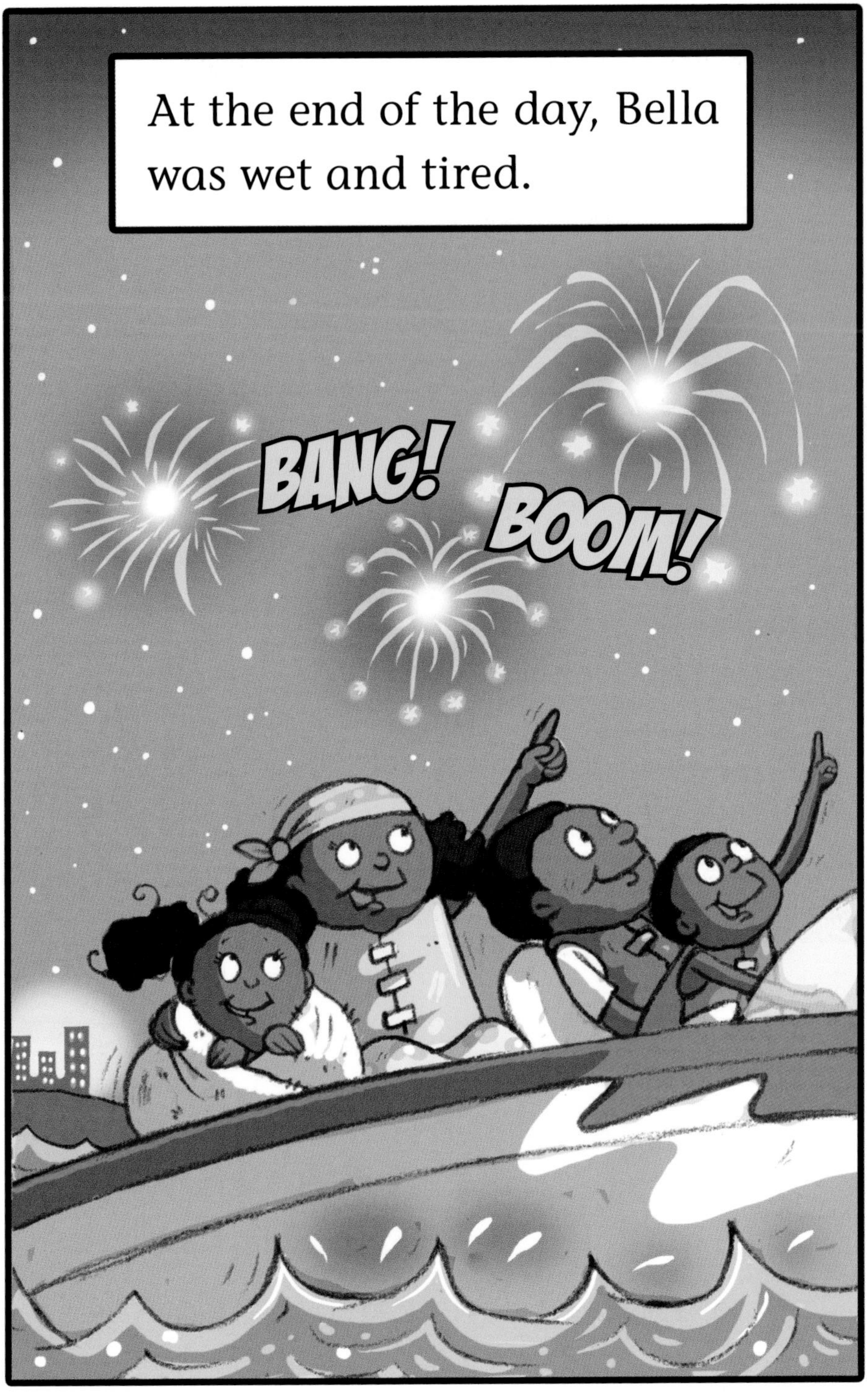
BANG!
BOOM!

Most of all, Bella was happy.

The End

ABOUT THE AUTHOR

Growing up in a small town with no cable TV (and parents who are teachers), reading was the only thing to do. Since then, Christianne Jones has read about a bazillion books and written more than 40. Christianne works as an editor and lives in Mankato, Minnesota, with her husband and daughter.

ABOUT THE ILLUSTRATOR

Mary Sullivan has been drawing and writing her whole life, which has mostly been spent in Texas. She earned a BFA from the University of Texas in Studio Art, but she considers herself a self-trained illustrator. Mary lives in Cedar Park, a suburb of Austin, Texas. She loves to go swimming in the lake with her dog.

GLOSSARY

cruise ship (KROOZ SHIP)—a big boat that carries passengers; usually used for vacations

dock (DOK)—a place where ships load and unload people and cargo

motorboat (MOH-tur-boht)—a small boat that has a motor

rowboat (ROH-boht)—a small boat that does not have a motor; a person must use oars to row it

sailboat (SAYL-boht)—a boat that moves by the wind blowing on its sails

DISCUSSION QUESTIONS

1.) Have you ever been on a boat? If so, what kind? If not, what kind would you like to go on?

2.) Bella was surprised by the motorboat. What type of boat did you think she would go on?

3.) In this story, Bella tries something new. Talk about something new that you've tried. Did you have fun?

WRITING PROMPTS

1.) There are a lot of different types of boats. Pick your favorite kind and draw a picture of it.

2.) Bella and her brother go tubing. Make a list of other activites that you can do with a boat.

3.) Throughout the book, there are sound and action words next to some of the pictures. Pick at least two of those words. Then write your own sentences using those words.

MY 1ST GRAPHIC NOVEL

THE 1ST STEP INTO GRAPHIC NOVELS

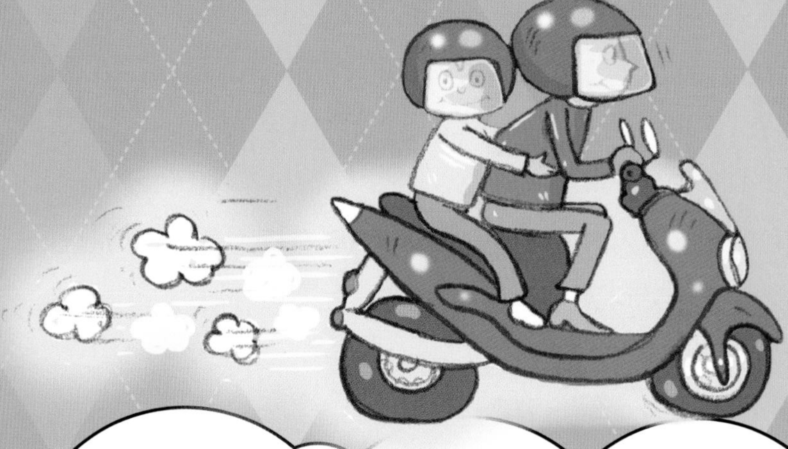

These books are the perfect introduction to graphic novels. Combine an entertaining story with comic book panels, exciting action elements, and bright colors, and a safe graphic novel is born.